Dear Parent:

Congratulations! Your child is taking the first steps on an exciting journey. The destination? Independent reading!

STEP INTO READING® will help your child get there. The program offers books at five levels that accompany children from their first attempts at reading to reading success. Each step includes fun stories, fiction and nonfiction, and colorful art. There are also Step into Reading Sticker Books, Step into Reading Math Readers, Step into Reading Write-In Readers, Step into Reading Phonics Readers, and Step into Reading Phonics First Steps! Boxed Sets—a complete literacy program with something to interest every child.

Learning to Read, Step by Step!

Ready to Read Preschool–Kindergarten
• big type and easy words • rhyme and rhythm • picture clues
For children who know the alphabet and are eager to begin reading.

Reading with Help   Preschool–Grade 1
• basic vocabulary • short sentences • simple stories
For children who recognize familiar words and sound out new words with help.

Reading on Your Own Grades 1–3
• engaging characters • easy-to-follow plots • popular topics
For children who are ready to read on their own.

Reading Paragraphs Grades 2–3
• challenging vocabulary • short paragraphs • exciting stories
For newly independent readers who read simple sentences with confidence.

Ready for Chapters Grades 2–4
• chapters • longer paragraphs • full-color art
For children who want to take the plunge into chapter books but still like colorful pictures.

STEP INTO READING® is designed to give every child a successful reading experience. The grade levels are only guides. Children can progress through the steps at their own speed, developing confidence in their reading, no matter what their grade.

Remember, a lifetime love of reading starts with a single step!

For Theo, the perfect pet for a princess
—M.L.

www.randomhouse.com/kids/disney

www.stepintoreading.com

Educators and librarians, for a variety of teaching tools, visit us at
www.randomhouse.com/teachers

Library of Congress Cataloging-in-Publication Data
Lagonegro, Melissa.
A pet for a princess / by Melissa Lagonegro ; illustrated by Atelier Philippe Harchy.
    p. cm. — (Step into reading. Step 2)
Summary: Princess Jasmine and her pet tiger become the best of friends.
ISBN 0-7364-2280-3 (pbk.)—ISBN 0-7364-8037-4 (lib. bdg.)
[1. Princesses—Fiction. 2. Tigers—Fiction.] I. Atelier Philippe Harchy. II. Title. III. Series.
PZ7.L14317 Pe 2005 [E]—dc22 2004003900

Printed in the United States of America   10 9 8 7 6 5 4

STEP INTO READING, RANDOM HOUSE, and the Random House colophon are registered trademarks
of Random House, Inc.

DISNEY PRINCESS

A Pet for a Princess

by Melissa Lagonegro
illustrated by Atelier Philippe Harchy

Random House 🏠 New York

Jasmine was
sad and lonely.
She needed a friend.

"Poor Jasmine,"
said her father.
"I want to make
you happy."

The next day,
he gave Jasmine
a big gift.
"Open it," he said.

Jasmine pulled off
the red sheet.

It was a tiger cub!

"I will call you Rajah,"
said Jasmine.
She was very happy.

Jasmine and Rajah
did many things
together.

They sat in the sun.

They watched butterflies.

They played
lots of games.

Jasmine took good care
of Rajah.

She fed him.

She brushed him.

She gave him

lots of love.

Jasmine liked
to rub and scratch
his furry belly.
Rajah liked it, too!
Purrrrr!

The princess kept Rajah
safe from harm.

And she loved to play
dress-up with him.

Jasmine made Rajah

a cozy little bed.

At night,

they fell fast asleep.

As time passed,

Rajah grew bigger . . .

and bigger . . .

. . . and bigger!

Rajah became
a <u>very</u> big tiger.
And a strong
tiger, too!

Now Rajah keeps
Jasmine safe
from harm.

Rajah is too big
to play dress-up.

He is too big
for his cozy little bed.

But he will never be

too big for a belly rub . . .

. . . or a hug!